ERIC CARLE

A House for Hermit Crab

READY-TO-READ

SIMON SPOTLIGHT

New York   London   Toronto   Sydney   New Delhi

This book was previously published with slightly different text.

For my son Rolf

SIMON SPOTLIGHT

An imprint of Simon & Schuster Children's Publishing Division

1230 Avenue of the Americas, New York, New York 10020

Copyright © 1987 Eric Carle Corporation

Eric Carle's name and signature logo type are registered trademarks of Eric Carle.

First Simon Spotlight Ready-to-Read edition 2014

For information about special discounts for bulk purchases, please contact Simon & Schuster Special Sales at

1-866-506-1949 or business@simonandschuster.com.

The Simon & Schuster Speakers Bureau can bring authors to your live event. For more information or to book an event

contact the Simon & Schuster Speakers Bureau at 1-866-248-3049 or visit our website at www.simonspeakers.com.

Manufactured in the United States of America 0414 LAK

First Edition 10 9 8 7 5 4 3 2 1

Library of Congress Cataloging-in-Publication Data

Carle, Eric.

A house for Hermit Crab / Eric Carle. — First edition.

pages cm. — (Ready-to-read. Level 2)

"First Simon Spotlight Ready-to-Read edition."

Originally published in a slightly different form by Picture Book Studio in Saxonville,

Massachusetts, 1987.

Summary: A hermit crab who has outgrown his old shell moves into a new one, which

he decorates and enhances with the various sea creatures he meets in his travels.

[1. Hermit crabs—Fiction. 2. Crabs—Fiction. 3. Marine animals—Fiction. 4. Dwellings—Fiction.] 1. Title.

PZ7.C21476Hp 2014

[E]—dc23

2013030571

ISBN 978-1-4814-0915-5 (pbk)

ISBN 978-1-4814-0916-2 (hc)

This book was previously published with slightly different text.

"It's time to move," said Hermit Crab
one day in January. "I've grown
too big for this little shell."

Hermit Crab had felt safe and snug
in his shell. But now it was too snug.
He stepped out of the shell
and onto the floor of the ocean.
But it was frightening out in the
open sea without a shell to hide in.

"What if a big fish comes along
and attacks me?" he thought.
"I must find a new house soon."

Early in February, Hermit Crab found
just the house he was looking for.
It was a big shell, and strong. He moved
right in, wiggling and waggling about
inside it to see how it felt. It felt just right.

"But it looks so—well, so *plain*,"
  thought Hermit Crab.

In March, Hermit Crab met some
sea anemones. They swayed gently
back and forth in the water.

"How beautiful you are!"
said Hermit Crab. "Would one of you
be willing to come and live on my
house? It is so plain, it needs you."

"I'll come," whispered a small
sea anemone.

Gently, Hermit Crab picked it up
with his claw and put it on his shell.

In April, Hermit Crab passed
a flock of starfish moving slowly
along the sea floor.

"How handsome you are!"
said Hermit Crab. "Would one of you
be willing to decorate my house?"

"I would," signaled a little sea star.
Hermit Crab picked it up
with his claw and put it on his house.

In May, Hermit Crab discovered
some coral. They were hard,
and didn't move.
"How pretty you are!"
said Hermit Crab. "Would one of you
be willing to help make my house
more beautiful?

"I would," creaked a crusty coral.
Carefully, Hermit Crab picked it up
with his claw and placed it
on his shell.

In June, Hermit Crab came upon
a group of snails crawling over a rock
on the ocean floor. They grazed
as they went, picking up algae
and bits of debris, and leaving
a neat path behind them.

"How tidy and hard-working you are!"
said Hermit Crab. "Would one of you
be willing to help clean my house?"

"I would," offered one of the snails.

Happily, Hermit Crab picked it up
with his claw and placed it on his shell.

In July, Hermit Crab came upon
several sea urchins. They had sharp,
prickly needles.
"How fierce you look!"
said Hermit Crab. "Would one of you
be willing to protect my house?"

"I would," answered a spiky sea urchin. Gratefully, Hermit Crab picked it up with his claw and placed it near his shell.

In August, Hermit Crab and his friends
wandered into a forest of seaweed.

"It's so dark here,"
thought Hermit Crab.
"How dim it is,"
murmured the sea anemone.
"How gloomy it is,"
whispered the starfish.
"How murky it is,"
complained the coral.
"I can't see!" said the snail.
"It's like nighttime!"
cried the sea urchin.

In September, Hermit Crab spotted
a school of lanternfish
darting through the dark water.
"How bright you are!" said Hermit Crab.
"Would one of you be willing
to light up our house?"

"I would," replied one lanternfish.
And it swam over near the shell.

In October, Hermit Crab
approached a pile of smooth pebbles.
"How sturdy you are!"
said Hermit Crab. "Would you mind
if I rearranged you?"

"Not at all," answered the pebbles.
Hermit Crab picked them up
one by one with his claw
and built a wall around his shell.
"Now my house is perfect!"
cheered Hermit Crab.

But in November, Hermit Crab
felt that his shell was a bit too small.
Little by little, over the year,
Hermit Crab had grown. Soon
he would have to find another,
bigger home.

But he had come to love his friends,
the sea anemone, the starfish,
the coral, the sea urchin, the snail,
the lanternfish, and even
the smooth pebbles.

"They have been so good to me,"
thought Hermit Crab. "They are like
a family. How can I ever leave them?"

In December, a smaller
hermit crab passed by.
"I have outgrown my shell," she said.
"Would you know of a place for me?"

"I have outgrown *my* house too,"
answered Hermit Crab. "I must
move on. You are welcome
to live here—but you must promise
to be good to my friends."

"I promise," said the little crab.

The following January, Hermit Crab
stepped out and the little crab
moved in.

"I couldn't stay in that little shell
forever," said Hermit Crab as he
waved goodbye.

The ocean floor looked wider than
he had remembered, but Hermit Crab
wasn't afraid. Soon he spied
the perfect house—a big, empty shell.
It looked, well, a little plain, but . . .

"Sponges!" he thought.
"Barnacles! Clown fish!
  Sand dollars! Electric eels! Oh,
  there are so many possibilities!
  I can't wait to get started!"

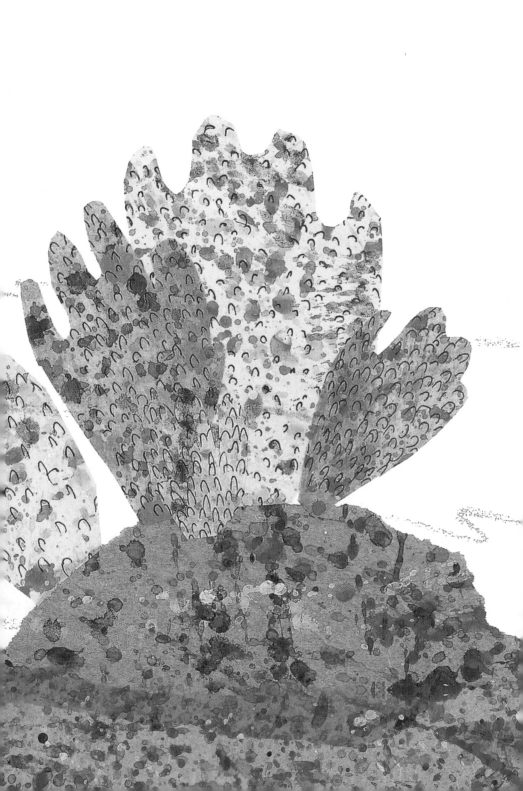

Sea Anemones may look like flowers, but they are soft animals (polyps) without bony skeletons. They come in many shapes and colors. With their many arms (tentacles) they catch their prey. Some specialize in attaching themselves to the shell of the hermit crab. Then they protect and camouflage the hermit crab, and, in turn, may share the hermit crab's meals. This arrangement is called symbiosis, meaning that both animals benefit from each other.

Starfish. There are many kinds of starfish. Most have five arms growing from a central disk. The mouth of a starfish is on the underside of this disk, and it has a single, simple eye at the end of each arm. With its powerful arms it can open an oyster, or hold onto a rock during a storm when the waves lash about.

Corals are somewhat similar to tiny sea anemones that build hard skeletons around themselves. Then hundreds and hundreds of them stick together, forming whole colonies. Some look like branches; others are round or disk-like. Millions upon millions fuse themselves together to build miles-long coral reefs. Some, however, live by themselves.

Snails. There are approximately 80,000 species of snails and slugs. Some live on land, others live in the sea or in lakes. Some carry a shell—their "houses"—on their backs; others have none. The shells come in many colors and shapes.

Sea Urchins. Some are fat and round, others are thin and spindly. Many have long spines (sometimes poisonous) with which they move around and dig into mud or rocks or other places. Their mouths, with five pointed teeth, are on the underside.

Lanternfish, like fireflies, have luminous, or light producing, spots on their bodies that light up their dark surroundings. Some lanternfish have a lantern-like organ that dangles in front of their mouths, attracting other fish which become their prey.